THE JIM FOREST READERS

Jim Forest and Ranger Don

Jim Forest and the Trapper

Jim Forest and the Ghost Town

Jim Forest and the Bandits

Jim Forest and Lightning

Jim Forest and Phantom Crater

Jim Forest and the Mystery Hunter

Jim Forest and the Plane Crash

Jim Forest and Dead Man's Peak

Jim Forest and the Flood

Jim Forest and Lone Wolf Gulch

Jim Forest and Woodman's Ridge

Jim Forest

and Woodman's Ridge

JOHN RAMBEAU
and
DOROTHEA GULLETT

Illustrations by JOSEPH MANISCALCO

Addison-Wesley Publishing Company, Inc.
Menlo Park, California • Reading, Massachusetts • London • Amsterdam
Don Mills, Ontario • Sydney

ISBN–0–201–40312–9
BCDEFGHIJK–VH–8107987

TABLE of CONTENTS

A Close Call

Jim Forest pulled his jacket closer and looked up at the sky. A cold, sharp wind cut through him like a knife. Even though it was summer, it was cool in the mountains. White clouds hung over Big Pines Forest.

Lining both sides of the road were big boulders. Jim looked at the two biggest ones. As long as the boy could remember, those two boulders had been there, as though standing watch over Eagle Pass. They rose, strong and silent, right into the clouds. Between them was a shiny, bright place in the sky.

"That's where the sun would be if there were no clouds," Jim thought to himself. "It must be almost time for lunch."

Jim turned toward his uncle. Jim's uncle was the forest ranger in Big Pines Forest. The ranger was studying a small pine branch.

"Uncle Don," Jim said as he nodded his head toward the sky, "isn't it almost time for lunch?"

The words had no sooner left his mouth than the boy was moving—and moving fast. At the same time he shouted, "Uncle Don, look out!"

Down the side of the mountain crashed a boulder. It smashed to a stop next to a tall pine. Smaller rocks came rolling down after the boulder.

"Jumping cats," said the ranger, looking at the rocks, "that was close!" The boulder had rolled to a stop at the very place where the ranger had been standing a minute before.

Jim didn't want his uncle to know how frightened he had been. "Oh, boy," he said, grinning, "just like television. The law was closing in on the cattle rustlers, so the rustlers pushed a boulder off the side of the mountain."

Jim pushed his hat down over his eyes. "I hope there won't be too much shooting. Where is my gun?"

The ranger laughed. "Now stop that! You know that there has been a lot of wind around here the last few days. Boulders are always rolling down the mountain. When you're at Eagle Pass, you have to be careful."

Bending down, he picked up the spray paint can that Jim had dropped. "Here is your gun, you clown! Now shoot this tree!"

"Yes, sir!" Jim answered, pushing his hat back in place.

The boy pointed the spray can and made a yellow mark across a white pine. Then he made a circle of yellow paint at the bottom of the tree. Later, when the loggers came, they would cut any tree that had been marked with yellow paint.

"Why does this tree have to be cut, Uncle Don?" asked Jim.

"It has blister rust, Jim."

Jim Forest knew about blister rust. Blister rust in a white pine forest means one thing —trouble! Carried by the wind, blister rust spreads from one white pine to another. It can spread through a whole forest of white pine in a very short time. Trees that have blister rust do not live very long.

The ranger walked through the trees, looking at the ground. At last he shouted, "I found them."

"Found what?" asked Jim. "The rustlers?"

"Don't be funny, Jim." The ranger pointed to some bushes. "I found these."

"Why, those are just gooseberry bushes," Jim said.

Ranger Don nodded his head. "Gooseberry bushes are a dangerous thing in a forest."

Jim laughed. "Uncle Don, *you* are being funny now."

The ranger shook his head. "No, Jim, I'm not being funny. Blister rust can live on gooseberry bushes before it spreads to the

trees. In order to stop the blister rust from spreading, these bushes will have to be taken out. I'll have to call the main ranger station for some men."

"What about the trees, Uncle Don?" Jim asked.

The ranger thought a minute. "Mr. Browne is logging on Woodman's Ridge. We'll drop by and tell him about them."

The ranger and Jim jumped into the truck and drove through Eagle Pass down to the main road. After a while the ranger turned west up the little winding road that would take them to Woodman's Ridge.

"This logging road sure isn't very wide," Jim said.

"You're right about that, Jim," Ranger Don said. "Two pickups can get by all right, but the road is just wide enough for one logging truck."

"What happens when a logging truck going down meets one coming up?" Jim shook his head at the thought.

The ranger laughed. "Don't worry about that. Only Mr. Browne uses this road, and he knows where all his logging trucks are."

At last they reached the logging camp. The ranger pulled his green pickup to a stop behind a big logging truck which was parked in the middle of the road. The logging truck blocked the whole road.

Standing next to the logging truck was a young man named Larry Grant. He worked for the rangers. He stayed at the camp to see that the loggers did a good, careful job. Larry also measured and marked every log that was taken out of the forest. Then the ranger would know how much money Mr. Browne would have to pay for the wood.

Larry Grant came over to the ranger. "Good to see you, sir," he said. He gave Jim a warm smile.

"Is Carl Browne around?" the ranger wanted to know.

"No, sir," Larry said, looking at his watch, "but it's almost one. He should be here by now."

Just then a pickup came up the road. The driver was Mr. Browne. Mr. Browne was a big man, one of the biggest that Jim had ever seen. When he saw the ranger, he waved. The shiny black pipe that he held in his mouth seemed to wave, too.

"It's about time you got to work, Carl," the ranger said, as Mr. Browne climbed out of the truck. The two men shook hands.

"I'm not as young as I used to be," Mr. Browne said. "I feel better if I sleep late."

While the men talked, Jim walked off. He didn't like the smell of Mr. Browne's pipe.

Jim walked up a small canyon to where the fallers were working. A faller is a man who fells, or cuts down, the trees. All the fallers were big, strong men.

Suddenly, one of the fallers turned off his power saw. He took off his hard hat and ran his hand across his face. Then he carried his saw down to a pickup truck. There he filled the saw with gas from a drum which was on the back of the truck.

Jim turned to watch some other loggers who were cutting up a tree that had already been felled. Jim knew that this tree was too long to be moved by truck. These men were cutting the tree into smaller parts. Then the man in the caterpillar would drag the logs down to the landing.

The landing was the area around the logging truck. There, Larry Grant would measure the logs to find out how wide and how long they were. After he marked them, the logs would be put on the logging truck.

Jim watched the loggers until the ranger was ready to go. As Jim climbed into the ranger's truck, Larry Grant and Mr. Browne were saying good-by.

"I'll be sending some men up here tonight to cut out those gooseberry bushes," the ranger said. "They will stay at the ranger's cabin at Eagle Pass. You'll be there in four days or so to cut out those white pines, is that right, Carl?"

Mr. Browne took his pipe out of his mouth. "That's right, ranger."

The ranger waved good-by, turned on the engine, backed the truck around, and started down the road.

Jim turned around to wave good-by again. Larry Grant smiled at him, but Mr. Browne was walking up the canyon, his hard hat on his head, ready for work.

Before Ranger Don and Jim had gone far, the ranger suddenly said, "Oh, I just remembered something that I wanted to tell Carl

Browne. Well, never mind, I'll tell him later."

"What is it?" Jim wanted to know.

"I wanted to tell him not to block the road with his logging truck," the ranger answered. "If there ever were a fire around here, the fire trucks would have to wait for Mr. Browne to move his truck. And, Jim, you know how important one minute is when there is a fire."

Jim nodded. In a strong wind a fire could spread over a whole ridge in minutes. Last summer Jim had been caught in a fire, and he knew how dangerous a fire was. He also knew the waste it left behind.

Looking around, Jim saw another kind of waste. This part of the forest had already been logged. In some places only a few trees had been taken out. But in other places whole areas had been logged.

"I wish we never had to cut trees, Uncle Don," Jim said.

"There are times trees have to be cut,

Jim," Ranger Don answered. "If they get blister rust—or something like it—they have to be cut down."

"But these trees didn't have blister rust," said Jim.

"You're right, they didn't." The ranger pointed to the right side of the road where all the trees had been cut down. "Before, that was a good stand of white pine, Jim. As you know, white pine is a very important timber tree. People like its wood. They pay a lot of money to get it. Those white pine trees will make a lot of money for Big Pines Forest—money that might be used for other parts of our forest.

"Now look over there, Jim. Only a few trees were cut down. That is a stand of ponderosa pine. Ponderosa pine does better if there aren't too many trees in one place.

"Trees, like most wild things, have to fight to live. Only the strong ones make it. We just helped a little by taking out the pines that were big enough to cut. Now the trees that are left will have a better chance.

"This part of the forest is good timber country, Jim, so it is used mainly for logging. But west of Woodman's Ridge is good grazing land because there aren't too many trees. The ranchers' cattle graze in that part of Big Pines. In other parts of the forest, there are bigger rivers, better-looking mountains—things that the people who come to Big Pines Forest want to see."

Jim knew that a lot of people came to Big Pines Forest during the summer. They came because they wanted to have fun and because they liked the mountains and trees.

Still, Jim wished that this part of Big Pines could be opened to the people, too.

Jim started to think about what he would do when he was a ranger. He almost wished he were a ranger now. He could hardly wait to get to forestry school.

When Ranger Don and Jim reached the

ranger station, they had a quick lunch. After that the ranger called the main ranger station at Two Rivers.

"We need some men to cut out those gooseberry bushes . . . All right . . . Great."

Then, from the look on the ranger's face, Jim could tell that something was wrong.

"Well," the ranger was saying, "I'll take the helicopter up tomorrow and look around . . . Friday . . . That's right . . . I'll call you tomorrow."

After the ranger hung up, he told Jim, "Two men to cut out the gooseberry bushes will be coming over in about an hour. That's all we could get. The others have to stand by. The rangers are worried about fire."

"Is that why you're worried?" Jim asked.

"I'm always worried about fire, Jim," Ranger Don answered, "but it seems we have other trouble, too. You know that the ranchers around Big Pines let their cattle graze in the forest during the summer. The other day, one of the ranchers went out to look over his cattle. He says that fifty head of his cattle have been stolen."

"Stolen!" Jim almost shouted. "That means there *are* cattle rustlers in Big Pines Forest. Maybe they did push that boulder—"

"Now, Jim, you have been watching too much television. No one pushed that boulder down on us. And that rancher's cattle might be lost, not stolen. Tomorrow, Friday, I will fly over Big Pines Forest in a helicopter. If by any chance there are cattle rustlers in this forest, I'll find them! And, Jim, I'm sending you up to Eagle Pass to help cut out those gooseberry bushes."

"Great, I'll like that!" Jim said out loud. To himself he added, "When I get to Eagle Pass, I am going to keep my eyes open. Maybe *I* will find the cattle rustlers!"

Jim Meets Murph

In one hour the two men from the main ranger station were supposed to pick Jim up. There wasn't much time to get ready. On the floor Jim spread out a blanket. He rolled up some warm clothes in it. Next he got some food. When the shiny truck from the main ranger station pulled to a stop in front, Jim was ready. At the sound of the horn, he ran out, threw his things in the back, and climbed in front.

Ranger Don was talking to the driver. "Jim," he said, "I want you to meet Sam Williams."

Jim reached over and gave his hand to the driver. Sam Williams had a warm, quick grin that made Jim like him right away. He was tan and good-looking. Even sitting down, he looked very tall.

"And this is Al Murphy," the ranger said, nodding to the boy who was sitting in the middle.

Jim tried not to, but he couldn't help staring. Al Murphy had the brightest red hair Jim had ever seen. He wasn't much older than Jim.

"I've heard that you have cut out gooseberry bushes before, Sam," Ranger Don said, "so I don't have to tell you too much about the job. Just make sure that you get all the gooseberry bushes cut out. If you leave just one bush, they will come right back up."

Sam nodded his head. "We just finished—" he started to say, when Al Murphy cut in.

"We just finished cutting out a big area of gooseberry bushes, sir," Al said in a friendly voice. "We understand how important this job is, and we'll be very careful."

"Good, Al—Sam," Ranger Don said.

Sam started the engine and stepped on the gas. Ranger Don moved back and waved good-by.

As the truck moved away from the ranger station, Al Murphy started laughing. "If that old man thinks I'm going to pull up a bunch of bushes, he's crazy!"

Sam grinned at Jim's surprised face and said, "Meet the *real* Murph, Jim."

Jim couldn't believe his ears. Was this the same boy who had been so friendly to his uncle just a few minutes before? When Jim found his voice, he said, "Old man—you mean my uncle?"

"Uncle — smuncle — old man, so what, sonny boy?" Murph laughed.

"Oh, no," Jim thought to himself, "*sonny boy!* Who does he think he is?"

"Why should I waste my time pulling up a bunch of bushes," Murph was saying. "Why waste your life watching over a bunch of trees? No, sir! Now, I don't mind watching over a bunch of money. Pull up bushes! Ha! That ranger must be crazy!"

"All right, Murph!" Sam's voice was sharp. "Be quiet for a while. You'll pull bushes, all right. That's what you're here for."

Murph went right on talking to Jim, just as if he had not heard. "Yeah, those rangers at Two Rivers think I'm a real square, and so does your uncle. Man, those rangers really fell for the line I handed them. Just as that old judge did! Yeah, that old judge thought he was really smart, sending me to work in this forest. But that judge isn't so smart as he thinks. I'm not going to do anything that I don't want to do."

Murph reached in his pocket and pulled out something. "See this?" he said. He opened his hand and showed Jim a pocket knife.

"Put that away, Murph!" Sam ordered. "Are you trying to frighten Jim?"

"No, chief, I was going to use it on you. Ha, ha, ha. That's crazy, man, crazy!"

Jim closed his eyes and put his head back. "Crazy is right!" he thought to himself. "A few days with Murph will drive *me* crazy."

Murph was talking on and on. He told about the last time he had been in trouble. One day he had cut school and had stolen a pickup truck.

"Yeah, the square who owned it had left it open. Man, was the truck something, a real cool job. I just got in and took off. Man, nothing could catch me!"

But the law had caught him. The judge had not wanted to send the boy to jail, so he had let him come to Big Pines Forest to work for the rangers.

Murph was laughing. "So what is wrong with jail? Five of my friends have been in jail. The judge said I might learn something in the forest. Ha, ha, ha. Learn what? There isn't anything that I don't already know. When it comes to stealing. . . ."

Jim tried not to listen. After a while Murph stopped talking about himself and looked at Jim. "Did you know that Sam's grandfather is an Indian—a real, live Indian? What does he do, Sam? I suppose he makes blankets on some Indian reservation? Ha, ha." Murph punched Jim in the ribs. "Look at old Chief-Red-in-the-Face!" he said.

Sam's tan grew dark and his brown eyes seemed to get black. "My grandfather does not make blankets," he said, his voice angry. "There is just one thing wrong with my grandfather. He does not like people with red hair."

Murph laughed, grabbed his own hair, and rolled his eyes. "Ha, ha! You really scare me."

It took only a few hours to drive to the cabin at Eagle Pass, but it seemed like days to Jim. Murph talked the whole time.

Jim was so happy to reach the cabin that he jumped out of the truck before it had come to a full stop. All he wanted to do was to get away from Murph's big mouth.

As Sam climbed out of the truck, he pointed above the cabin. There, in the west, the sun was a big ball of fire.

"Look at that red sun!" Sam said. "As my grandfather would say, tomorrow will be a good day."

Sam took some things out of the pickup and handed them to Murph and Jim. "You two start putting these things away," he said.

Jim started toward the cabin, his arms full of blankets. "Look!" he suddenly shouted. He tried to point at the same time. "The door to the cabin is broken!"

Sam rushed to the door, pushed it open, and looked inside the cabin. Behind him, Jim looked, too.

"From the looks of the place, someone has been living here," Sam said.

Bunks lined two walls of the small cabin. Hanging out of the bunks were clothes and blankets. Against another wall stood a sink. Covering the sink were opened cans of food.

Jim dropped the blankets he was carrying down on a bunk. "My uncle told me that there might be some cattle rustlers working in Big Pines Forest. You don't suppose the cattle rustlers could have been staying here!"

"I don't know," Sam said. "Anyone could have broken in here." Sam thought a minute. Then he said, "You two get to work in here. I'll go out and look around."

Jim picked a cup off the floor and threw it in the sink.

Murph, his hands in his pockets, was looking around. "What a drag!" he said, sinking down on a bunk. "No radio—no television. What are we going to do for fun?"

"I'm sure you'll think of something," said Jim. "But until you do, how about helping me put away some of these things?"

"Go right ahead, sonny boy. You are doing a good job all alone. I'll just watch and make sure you keep it up."

Jim put down the can of food he was holding and turned around. "I think you should help, Murph."

Murph grinned. "Oh, you do! Well, why don't you make me? Come on, I'm waiting. Are you afraid?"

Jim took another step, his eyes angry.

Murph's grin grew even bigger. "Hey, sonny boy, and I do mean *boy,* do you really think you can take me?"

Though Murph was just a little taller than Jim, he was a lot bigger. But Jim felt that he had to do something. If he didn't stand up against Murph, Murph would walk all over

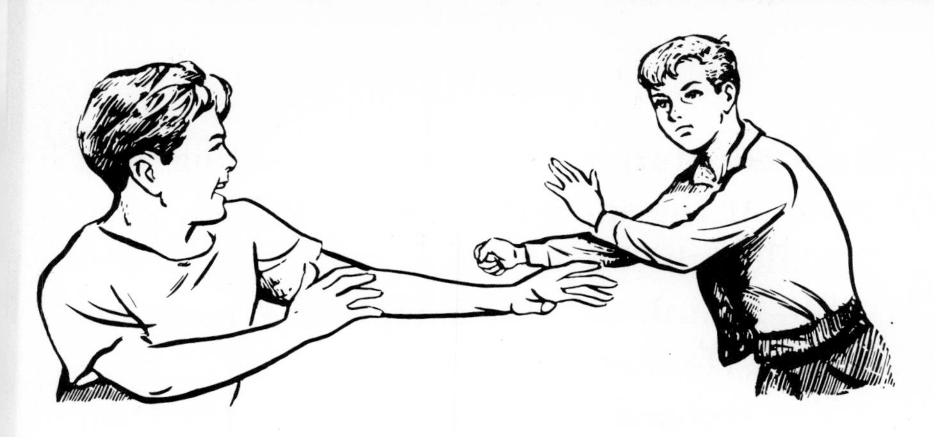

him. Not only that, there was nothing that Jim wanted to do more than to punch Murph in the chin.

Suddenly Murph swung his legs off the bunk and sat up.

Jim moved closer. When Jim was a step away, Murph, who was still smiling, stood up.

Jim put up his right hand and threw a hard left toward Murph's chin. The grin never left Murph's face. The redhead reached over, grabbed Jim's arm, and swung hard. Before Jim knew what was happening, his feet went out from under him, and he was on his back in the middle of the floor.

Just then Sam rushed inside the cabin. He dropped the books he was carrying and grabbed Murph by the neck, pulling him back. At the same time he asked Jim, "Are you all right?"

"I—I think so," Jim said, trying to get his breath. He slowly got to his feet.

The redhead was trying to get away from Sam's strong hold. Sam didn't even look at him. He just went on talking to Jim. "I should have told you that Murph knows judo. But so do I, don't I, Murph?"

Murph could not talk. He couldn't even move his head.

"If you ever again pull judo on someone smaller than you, I'll show you an old Indian trick or two."

Sam's eyes never left Murph's face. Under Sam's sharp look, the redhead had to drop his eyes.

Sam let Murph go and stood back. "All right, both of you, get to work."

Bending over, Sam started to pick up his books. "Did you boys find anything?"

Jim held up a jacket. "One thing I know—only men were staying here. All these clothes are men's."

Sam looked around. "Jim, you know this cabin better than we do. Has anything been stolen?"

"Not that I can see." Jim pointed to the far wall. "All the fire-fighting tools are there, as well as the things we'll need to cut out gooseberry bushes tomorrow."

"I looked around the cabin, but I couldn't find any tire tracks," Sam said. "We're going to have to keep our ears open as long as we stay here."

Later that night, long after Sam and Murph had gone to sleep, Jim lay on his bunk, thinking. He was sure that the men who had been staying in the cabin were the cattle rustlers.

"I'm going to stay up all night and listen," he thought to himself. "Those cattle rustlers will be back here. I just know it!"

A Truck Comes to Eagle Pass

Murph had hold of Jim's neck. He was pulling and pulling. Jim felt the ground rock. Then, as though from far away, he heard a voice.

"Wake up, Jim, wake up!" the voice said.

Jim shook his head and opened his eyes. It wasn't Murph at all—just Sam, standing over him, trying to wake him up.

"Wh—what is it?" Jim asked.

"Get up, Jim!"

"Go away, I'm sleeping. It's not light enough to cut gooseberry bushes."

"Jim, you must get up. I hear an engine."

Jim sat up, listening, his eyes wide. "Do you think the cattle rustlers might be coming here?" he asked.

"Someone might. I think we should go out and watch."

Sam turned toward Murph's bunk. Murph was staring at them.

"I think you're both crazy," the redhead said. "Go ahead—waste your time running around in the middle of the night, looking for a bunch of cattle rustlers. I'm going back to sleep!"

"Oh, no, you aren't!" Sam said. "You're not staying here alone."

Murph turned his back on them, lay down on the bunk, and pulled the blanket up to his chin.

Sam's eyes got dark. "Put your clothes on," he ordered, "or I'll put them on you."

"All right, all right." Murph put one leg on the floor. "You don't have to get tough!"

Jim and Murph pulled on their clothes and followed Sam out of the cabin. It was so dark that they could not see a thing.

Sam showed them how to cup their hands around their eyes.

"You'll see better that way," Sam said in a low voice. "That's the way Indians see in the dark."

"Why not just use a flashlight?" Murph's voice was loud.

"Quiet!" Sam whispered back. He was silent for a minute, but then he went on. "Use your head, Murph. I have a flashlight with me, but if I turn it on, someone might see the light. Now follow me and be as quiet as you can. Remember that sounds carry a long way in the night!"

Cupping his hands around his eyes, Jim followed Sam. He wished there were a full moon so that he could see better. He looked behind him. He couldn't see Murph, though he knew that the redhead was not too far away.

Then Sam stopped so suddenly that Jim bumped into him.

"What is that in your jacket pocket?" Sam whispered. "It feels like a gun."

"Sure, I'm going to shoot the rustlers," said Jim, smiling. "It's really a can of spray paint, which I used today while marking trees."

Sam turned his head to the side, listening. "Come on," he whispered, "let's cut into the forest."

Once off the road, walking was much harder. The forest floor lay covered with pine needles and dry leaves. Little rocks rolled under Jim's feet. Ahead, Sam moved on, quickly and silently. Behind was Murph, just as quiet. To Jim, it seemed that he was the only one making any noise.

When they were almost to the place where Jim and his uncle had been marking trees that morning, Sam stopped. From behind some big boulders, the boys watched. Jim couldn't see a thing, but he could hear the sound of an engine getting closer and closer. It sounded like a truck's engine.

As Jim waited, his mind moved quickly. This had to be the cattle rustlers! It couldn't be tourists. Few tourists came to this part of the forest because this was logging country. On the other hand, cattle rustlers would be sure to know that. They would know that they could drive around in this area at night without being heard or seen.

Then Jim remembered another thing. Not far from here, on the other side of Woodman's Ridge, the ranchers' cattle grazed. The cabin at Eagle Pass would be a good place for cattle rustlers to hang out.

Then suddenly the forest was silent. The truck had stopped—and not far from where the boys watched.

Then Murph did a funny thing. One minute he was at Jim's side. The next, he was creeping off through the forest.

Sam whispered, "Hey, where are you going? Come back here!"

Murph gave no sign that he heard.

Sam started to go after Murph, but then he changed his mind. From the road came sounds of low voices!

As the minutes went by, the sounds from the road got louder and louder.

Jim took a deep breath and stepped back. As he did, there was a loud noise. Jim had stepped on a dry branch!

"Hey," someone shouted, "did you hear something?"

Then Jim heard the men crashing through the forest toward him and Sam.

"Boy, are we in trouble," Jim thought.

Sam pulled Jim down to the ground. Not far ahead was a small, bright light. The shiny light was a flashlight that was coming closer and closer.

Jim thought that at any minute the light would point him and Sam out. He wanted to jump up and run away, but he lay still.

Now the light was so close that Jim was afraid to take a breath.

Suddenly, the man carrying the flashlight shouted, "There he is!"

Jim closed his eyes, waiting for what would happen next.

"I see him—over by that tree!" the same man called out.

Jim's eyes opened. The two men went running by Sam and him.

Jim looked up the road. In the light from the flashlight, Jim saw a man wearing a blue jacket. The man ran between some trees at the side of the road. Jim could hear him crashing through the forest. The two men ran after him.

When they had gone, Sam grabbed Jim's arm and pulled him up.

"Let's get out of here," Sam whispered.

Sam and Jim moved deeper into the forest. They had not gone far when Sam stopped. The engine had started, and the truck was moving down the road.

After a while Sam said, "That truck is going back down the mountain."

Jim took a deep breath. "Who were those two men with the flashlight? And who was that other man—the man in the blue jacket?"

"I don't know that, Jim. I just know that those two men were just as surprised to see that man in the blue jacket as he was to see them. Did you see the way he took off?"

Jim nodded. "What were they all doing here? You don't suppose they came here to watch us, do you? And what about Murph? Where do you suppose Murph went?"

"I have no idea!" Sam's voice was angry. "Isn't that just like him—running off at a time like this! Come on, Jim, I suppose we should look for him. We'll have to take a chance and turn on this flashlight."

Bending down, Sam looked for Murph's tracks.

"Hey, watch out!" Jim called just as Sam was about to walk into a tree. "The Indians on television are able to track people without bumping into trees, so why can't you?"

Sam grinned back. "Stop worrying about me and start calling Murph."

While Jim shouted Murph's name, Sam looked around. At last Sam said, "No use kidding you, Jim, I can't find anything."

"I have it!" Jim said. "Maybe Murph went back to the cabin. He didn't want to come with us in the first place, remember?"

"That would be just like him," Sam said, "in the cabin sleeping, while we're out here looking." Sam made his voice sound like Murph's. " 'Two squares!' he would call us—and he would be right!"

As they walked toward the cabin, Jim thought about all the things that had happened. When the two men had run by, there had been something about them. Jim had not seen the men at all. One man had held the flashlight in front of him. Most of the time the light had been in Jim's eyes.

Jim told Sam what he was thinking. "And there is something about the men that makes me feel that I know them."

"You keep thinking about it, Jim," Sam said. "Maybe you'll remember. I've been thinking that we should let your uncle know about the men and that truck."

Jim nodded his head. "We can call my uncle on the two-way radio in the pickup."

Minutes later, Sam and Jim were back at the cabin. They rushed over to the truck, and Sam pulled the door open.

"I don't think we'll be calling anyone," Sam said. "Look, Jim, the radio has been smashed!"

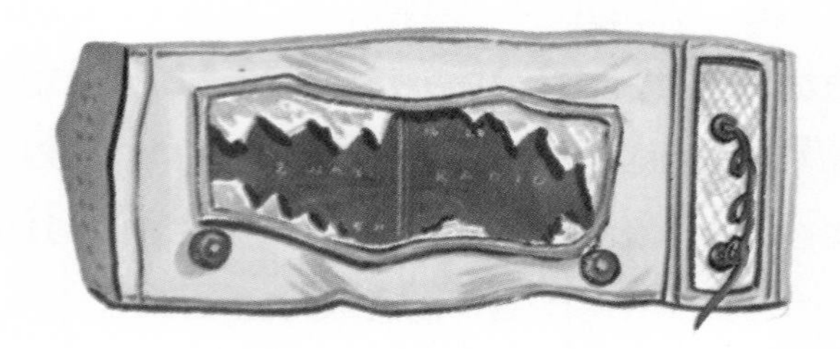

Going for Help

Jim stared at the smashed radio, but he could hardly believe his eyes. Who could have done it? Then he turned to Sam. "Do you think Murph smashed this radio?"

Sam said, "I don't know, Jim. He had a chance to come back here and do it, all right. It would be just like him, too. Let's take a look in the cabin."

Jim and Sam went inside the cabin and looked around. Then Jim grabbed Sam's arm and pointed to the place above the sink where he had put all their food. Not one can was left!

"Do you think Murph would take all our food?" Jim wanted to know.

Sam looked around. "He could have, Jim, but why wouldn't he take all his clothes, too? And Jim, there on my bunk!"

Jim looked. At the head of Sam's bunk lay Murph's knife! It was open!

"His knife, Jim! There is Murph's knife. Murph was crazy about that knife. He just would not leave it here. It must be some kind of sign, but what?"

"If Murph didn't take the food, then someone did. That means Murph could be in danger. What are we going to do? Do you think we should look for him again?"

"Let's face it, Jim. I'm not very good at tracking. In order to find him, we'll need a lot of people to help look for him. I don't think that two of us can do much good."

"You're right, Sam. We need help, and fast. If Murph gets lost in the forest, he will be in real danger!"

Sam nodded toward the truck. "I think we should drive down to the ranger station and tell your uncle what has happened."

Minutes later, Sam and Jim were in the truck, heading down the mountain toward the ranger station. Jim was so tired he could hardly keep his eyes open. He had not had more than an hour's sleep. Not only that, he was hungry, too.

The truck had gone only four or five miles when the engine started coughing.

"Something is wrong," Sam said. He parked the truck at the side of the road and got out. He lifted the hood and looked at the engine.

Jim watched as Sam worked on the engine. Then he asked, "Do you want to be a mechanic? You know a lot about engines."

"No, Jim, I don't want to be a mechanic, but my grandfather is one. I learned a lot about engines just by watching him." Sam smiled at the look on Jim's face.

"My grandfather and I live in a city. Murph likes to think we live on a reservation, so I let him. He has a funny idea that there is something wrong in living on a reservation."

Jim shook his head. "I think Murph has a lot of funny ideas. He's the creep, not us."

Sam gave Jim the flashlight. "Point the light over here, Jim."

Jim moved the flashlight where he was told. At last Sam shook his head. "I don't see anything wrong," he said.

Sam got back in the truck and tried to start it again. The engine turned over, but it would not start.

Jim was still standing by the door. "I'm no mechanic," he said, looking inside the truck, "but I can tell you what is wrong. We're out of gas!"

"Out of gas!" Sam said in surprise. "But how can that be? I filled the tank in Two Rivers, just before I picked you up."

Sam got out of the truck again and looked into the gas tank. After a few minutes he said, "You're right, Jim. Someone has drained the tank. There was just enough gas left in the tank to get us here."

"Well," Jim said, "if you want to get to the ranger station, we'll have to—"

"I know—walk!" Sam grinned. "How far would you say it is to the ranger station?"

"It's only about fifty miles," Jim answered.

Sam thought a minute. "Well, a man walks around four miles an hour, so it should take us—"

Jim broke in, "We might bump into some tourists before we walk the whole fifty miles. But wait a minute! I have an idea! Mr. Browne is logging near here. His camp is on Woodman's Ridge. We could walk there in a few hours. By that time it should be light, and Mr. Browne's loggers will be at work."

"That's good thinking, Jim. We'll be able to get some help there."

Jim pointed west. "Let's cut across the mountain. It will be shorter than going by road."

As Sam and Jim climbed up the mountain, the sky grew light. It was quiet in the forest. The only sound was the whisper of wind through the trees. The smell of pine hung in the air.

"I'm crazy about this country, Jim," Sam said, taking a deep breath. "Smell that air! Isn't it great? I want to live in a place like this some day. That's why I'm studying forestry in school. Some day I am going to be a forest ranger, just like your uncle."

"I'm going to study forestry, too," Jim said.

The mountain was getting steeper. Jim and Sam stopped talking and just climbed. After a while they stopped and sat down to get their breath.

"When I was a little kid, there was a tree that looked a lot like that one in a park not far from where I lived." Sam pointed to a tall pine tree. "I always wanted to climb it, so one day I did. I got up but I couldn't get down. I stayed up that tree all night, hanging on, afraid to move. When morning came, I climbed down." Sam laughed. "Well, I really didn't climb down. As I remember, I fell out of it."

Sam stopped talking. "It sure was a great tree," he added after a while. "Murph does not understand about trees." Sam fell silent again.

Jim knew how Sam felt about trees. He felt the same way himself. Every once in a while, he saw a tree that some tourist had cut his name in. Every time Jim saw that, he would get angry. He didn't understand why people did things like that.

Sam started talking again. "I understand Murph, but still I get angry at him. I know he's had a tough life. Where he grew up, he had to be strong. He had to be tough."

"Other people have had it tough, too, but they don't try to push people around the way Murph does," Jim said.

"You're right, Jim. Murph has a lot to learn. And there is something you have to learn, too, Jim. That's judo. You have to show Murph up at his own game. And Murph's game is judo. If you knew some judo, Murph would leave you alone. Would you like me to show you a few throws?"

"Yes!" Jim said, jumping up.

Sam laughed. "Not now! But I will—later. First, let's find Mr. Browne's logging camp."

A few hours later Sam and Jim were at the bottom of a deep canyon. A river cut across the bottom.

Sam shook his head. "You and your short cuts," he said. "I think we would have made better time if we had stayed on the road. Woodman's Ridge is on the other side of the river. It looks like the only way we're going to get across it is to swim."

Jim grinned. "Let's follow the river downstream for a while. We might find a way to cross without getting wet."

They walked along the river, looking for a place to cross. Not far downstream, they found a log that had been felled by the wind. It lay across the river. Being careful not to slip, Sam and Jim walked across the log to the other side of the river.

"Nothing to it!" Jim said, smiling. "I told you I would find a way." Jim looked up at the sky. "I thought you said last night when you saw the red sun that today would be a good day. Just look at those clouds!"

Sam grinned. "Just wait, Jim, just wait. The day might turn out to be a good one after all." He stopped talking and lifted his hand. "Hey, Jim, listen. What did I tell you about this being a good day? Do you hear what I hear?"

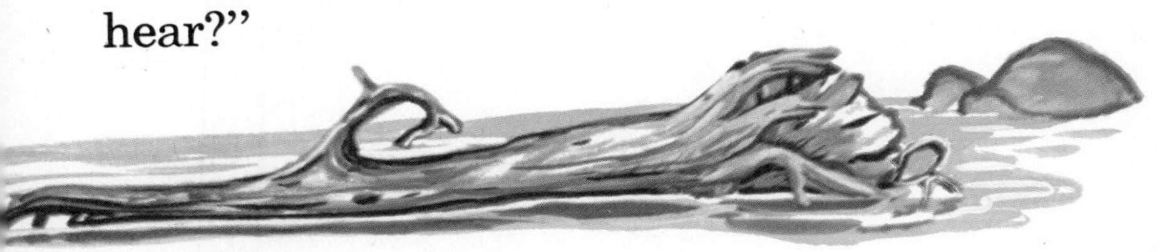

Smoke and Clouds

It was Murph! Jim could hear his voice.

"Help! Help!" Murph was calling.

Jim and Sam hurried over the rocks. The going was rough. Big boulders lined both sides of the river. Then the river made a sharp turn to the right. Once around the bend, Sam and Jim stopped.

On the other side of the river, his back against a boulder, was Murph. He didn't seem at all surprised to see them. He looked as though he were waiting for them.

"Where have you been, and what are you doing there?" Sam wanted to know.

"I'm getting a sun tan, chief, what do you think? I've heard you two squares crashing around out there for the last hour. It's about time you got here! Now will you creeps get me out of here?"

"How did you ever get over there in the first place?" Sam asked as he studied the area.

All around Murph, making a wall of rock, were tall steep boulders. There wasn't any way that Murph could get around them. Above his head there were more rocks.

"I was climbing up the mountain," the redhead pointed in back of him. "I slipped on some pine needles, fell, and rolled into this place. I've been here for hours. Now are you going to do something?"

"Why didn't you swim across the river?" Sam wanted to know.

"And get wet? Are you crazy?"

"Well, you'll have to, Murph. That's the only way you'll get out." Jim pointed to the rocks. "There is no way to get around those."

"Don't you think I know that, sonny boy?"

"Come on, Murph, you'll have to swim across," Sam said.

Murph shook his head. "Not on your life!"

"All right then," Sam said and turned to Jim, "let's go!"

Jim grinned, and he and Sam started downstream again.

"Hey," Murph cried and got to his feet. "You're not going to leave me here, are you? Hey, you two, come back!"

Sam stopped and turned. "Well, are you going to swim across?"

"I can't swim, you creeps—that's why I can't get across. I can't swim." Murph sat back down. "So go on—leave me here."

"Why didn't you tell us that before?" Sam said.

Sam looked down at the water, which was moving fast. He could see the rocks at the bottom. With his eyes, he measured how far it was across the river. The river was not wide, but it was deep—deep and cold.

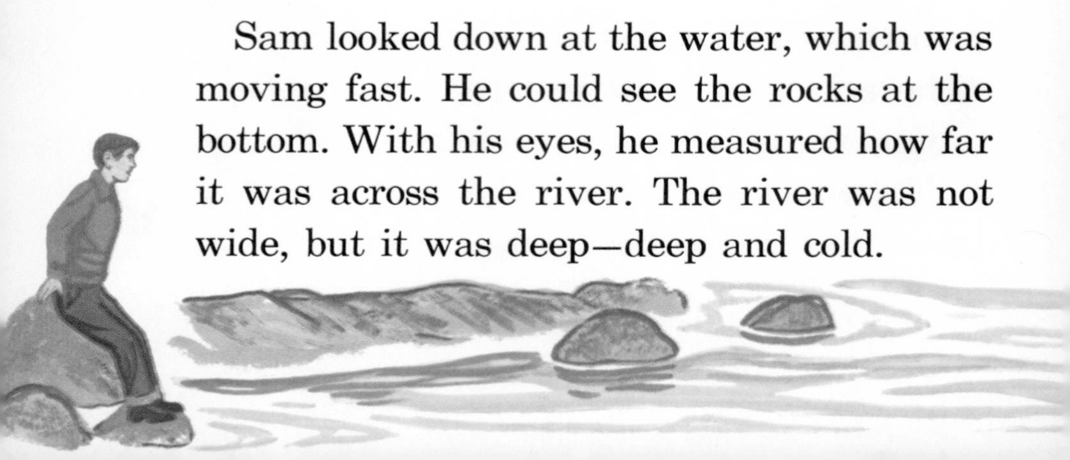

"I'll have to come over there and get you," Sam said at last. "But you'll have to do what I say."

"Wait a minute, Sam," Jim said. "You're not thinking about swimming back with Murph? You can't. It's too dangerous."

"I have to. We can't leave Murph there."

Sam started to take off his jacket. "You better take off your jacket, Murph. Roll it up and try to throw it over here."

Murph did as he was told. He rolled his jacket into a ball, but his throw was too short, and his jacket landed in the river. Sam reached out and grabbed it before the river could carry it downstream.

"Here," Sam said, handing the wet jacket to Jim, "get a fire going, and dry this. I'm going after Murph."

Sam stepped into the water. "This water is so cold, I'm turning blue already!"

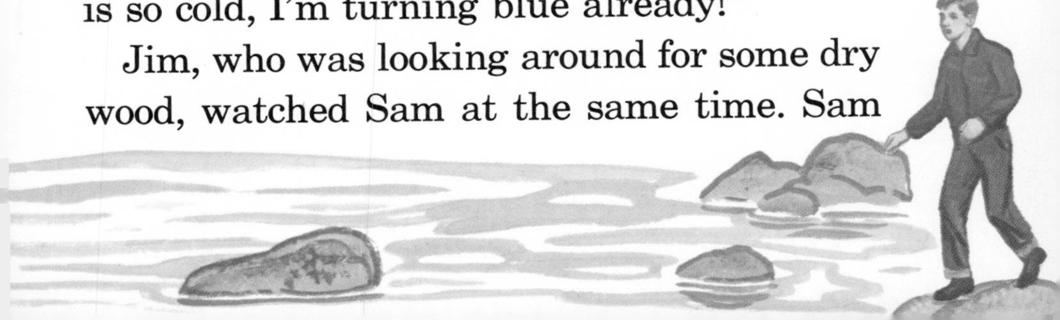

Jim, who was looking around for some dry wood, watched Sam at the same time. Sam

was swimming. In a minute he had reached the other side.

"I'll pull you across, Murph," Sam said, "but you're going to have to lie back in the water." Sam showed Murph how. "I know it is hard, but you'll have to do it. Most important of all, you must not fight me. If you do, we'll both go under."

Sam put his arm under Murph's chin, and started to swim back. Murph's eyes showed that he was frightened, but he lay still. In a minute Sam had pulled Murph to the other side.

For a while no one said anything. Then Sam said, "Hurry up with that fire, Jim. We're cold." Then he turned to Murph.

"That was really something, Murph. Not many people could lie back in the water like that and not fight!"

For a minute the tough look on Murph's face left, but then it came back. "What do you creeps think I am?" Murph said. "I never get scared! You should have seen the time I stole a pickup! Man, the law—"

"Oh, no!" Jim said, turning to Sam. "Can't we make him be still?"

"Murph, you have said enough. You open that big mouth of yours once more, and I'll throw you into the river! Now be quiet!" Sam said. "Get those wet things off, too."

Next to a tall boulder, Jim had a good fire going. He warmed his hands over it as Murph got out of his wet clothes.

"Oh, what happened to you?" Jim stared at Murph's side. It was black and blue!

"You sure had some fall," Sam said. He gave Murph a sharp look. "You might have some broken ribs."

Just then Jim jumped up. "Listen," he shouted, "I hear something."

As they listened, the noise from a helicopter came closer and closer. "Now I remember! My uncle said he was going to fly over Big Pines Forest on Friday. And today is Friday. But look!" Jim pointed to the sky. "The clouds are still low. Uncle Don will never see us at the bottom of this ridge."

"Quick," Sam said. "Get some wet wood and throw it on the fire. That will make a lot of smoke."

Jim and Sam rushed around, picking up wood and throwing it on the fire. They put more and more wood on the fire. Great clouds of smoke rose into the air. There was so much smoke that soon Sam and the boys were coughing. Every time Murph coughed, he held his side in pain.

Jim looked up. Would his uncle see the smoke? Or from the helicopter, would the smoke look like a cloud?

Rustlers

Silently Sam, Jim, and Murph watched the smoke as it rose into the clouds. At last Jim shook his head.

"It's no use," he said. "The helicopter is leaving. My uncle couldn't see the smoke through these clouds."

Sam pulled the wet wood out of the fire and started putting dry wood in its place. As he worked over the fire, he said, "How about it Murph? Where have you been? Why did you take off last night?"

Murph held his hands over the fire. "I suppose I should tell you two squares, but I don't know why." Murph shook his head. "You two go creeping through the forest after some truck that just happens to drive up the road. There you are—all big-eyed and worried about a truck—while the real thieves walk right by you."

"You mean," Jim said, "you found the cattle rustlers? Then the men in the truck were not cattle rustlers!"

"You are right, sonny boy," Murph said. "Yeah! It takes a thief to catch a thief, I always say. You just have to be a bigger and better thief to—"

"But what about the cattle rustlers?" Sam broke in.

"Yes, I want to know about that, too," said Jim.

"Yeah," Murph said. "As I was saying, the two cattle rustlers almost bumped into you."

"Was one of the cattle rustlers wearing a blue jacket?" Sam wanted to know.

"Yeah," Murph said. "That was one of them. The other man was wearing a brown jacket with a hood—and he's the one I followed!"

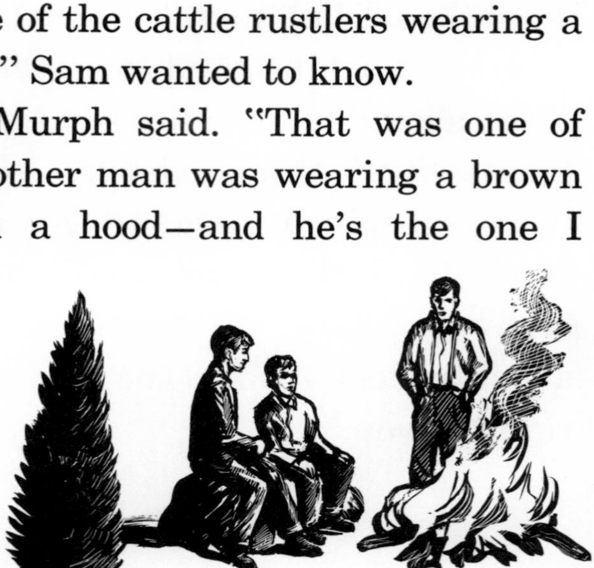

"Good thinking, Murph," Sam said. "Did you find out what the cattle rustlers were doing at Eagle Pass?"

Murph nodded. "They had been staying at the cabin. Then last night they found us. They were trying to think of a way to get our food when they heard the truck. They went back up the road, and one of them stayed to watch the truck. When the other man came back to the cabin he—"

Sam broke in, "Then he's the one who smashed the radio and drained the gas tank."

"And took all our food," Jim said.

Murph nodded. "When he took off with our food, I slipped into the cabin and threw my knife on the bunk. Sam, you're supposed to be good at understanding Indian signs. I left the knife pointing up the road. Did you find the tracks I left for you to follow?"

Sam laughed and shook his head. "It looks like you're the only one who knows anything about tracking. How did you learn?"

"It's nothing, man! In my game, you have to have eyes and legs like a cat. You have to be able to see in the dark and to move around without being heard or seen. If not"—Murph threw up his hands—"the next thing you know you're sitting in jail, wondering what happened! Well, as I was saying, I followed the rustler. Not far from the cabin, the man in the blue jacket was waiting. I could hear him talking. He said that he had almost been caught by two men in a truck."

"We saw it happen," Jim said.

"Do the cattle rustlers know who the men in the truck were?" Sam wanted to know.

Murph shook his head. "No, they think the men in the truck might have been rangers."

Sam looked at Jim. "Remember last night you said you thought you knew one of the men. Do you think one was a ranger?"

"I—I don't think so," Jim answered slowly.

"Well, I followed the two rustlers to Woodman's Ridge," Murph went on. "Now that we are staying at the cabin, the rustlers are camping out next to a little canyon where they are keeping the cattle."

"You did a good job, Murph," Sam said. "The rangers will be very happy to hear about this."

Then Jim thought about something. "Why are the cattle rustlers waiting in Big Pines? Isn't it dangerous? They have the cattle. Why don't they just truck the cattle out of the forest?"

"I know why," Murph said. "The only time they can move the cattle out of the forest is during the night. But they can't get out of Big Pines Forest at night because some people are cutting timber. The cattle rustlers can't get the cattle by the logging camp."

"Cutting timber?" Jim didn't seem to understand.

"Yeah," Murph said. "Some man named Browne is logging at night."

"Browne—logging at night! I don't believe you," Jim said.

"Believe me—don't believe me. It's all the same to me. I should waste my breath talking to you."

Jim turned to Sam. "There is something funny about this," he said. "Mr. Browne can't be logging at night. Logging at night is against the law."

"So this Browne is stealing," Murph put in. "So what!"

"I just can't believe it," Jim said. "Mr. Browne has worked here for a long time. I know him! He just couldn't be a thief."

Sam put his hand on Jim's arm. "I know Mr. Browne is your friend, but think, Jim. Think back to last night. You said there was something about those men that made you think you knew them. Do you remember what it was?"

Jim closed his eyes and thought back to the night before. He had been on the ground, watching the flashlight come closer and closer. He was so frightened that he had closed his eyes. He couldn't see anything, but he could hear the men crashing toward him. Even now he could hear the men as they came nearer. He could almost smell the pine and smell the—

Jim jumped to his feet! "I've got it," he shouted. "I smelled smoke! The man wasn't smoking then, but the smell was on his clothes. And Carl Browne smokes a pipe!"

"So one of the men in the truck was Carl Browne," Sam said. "But what was he doing at Eagle Pass? What could he have wanted?"

"I don't know," Jim said, "but I just remembered something. When my uncle and I were at Mr. Browne's logging camp the other day, I remember that Mr. Browne's big logging truck was blocking the road so that nothing could get by it."

"Sure," Sam said. "I get it! Mr. Browne keeps that road blocked so that no one can get up it without his knowing it."

"Right, man!" Murph said. "But what Browne does not know is that the cattle rustlers can't get *down* it!"

Sam held his hand to his mouth, and Murph stopped talking.

" I hear something!" Sam said.

"Power saws!" Jim said. "That is the sound of power saws. Mr. Browne's logging camp must not be too far from here. What are we going to do?"

Jim sat down. All at once he was more tired and hungry than he had ever been in his whole life.

As though he knew what Jim was thinking, Murph suddenly said, "Are you two hungry?"

"Hungry! Don't say that word," Jim said. "I can't stand it."

Murph laughed. "Once a thief, always a thief," he added.

Jim wondered what Murph was getting at.

Sam, who was staring at Murph, suddenly started grinning. "Why, you thieving red-head!" he shouted.

Jim looked at Sam and Murph in wonder. They were both laughing. All along, Jim had been sure that Murph was crazy, but now had Sam lost his mind, too? Maybe it was catching, and in a few hours, he would be crazy, too.

Sam threw Jim a quick grin. "Don't you understand what has happened? Murph stole the food back from the thieves!"

Murph grinned. "No thief is going to steal something from me and get away with it. I sure would like to see the look on those two men's faces when they get up this morning and look for the food they stole from us. Why, when it comes to stealing, I'm the best—"

"Never mind that!" Sam said. "Where is it, Murph?"

Murph nodded toward the river. "The food is on the other side of the river. When I slipped on those pine needles and started rolling down the mountain, I dropped it. It should be—yeah! There it is." Murph finished by pointing to something brown on the side of the mountain. It was a blanket full of food.

Jim no longer felt tired. "I'll go," he said, jumping up.

"Don't slip on those pine needles!" Sam shouted after him.

Jim made his way back up the river to the log he and Sam had crossed. In no time at

all he had found the food and was back at the fire. He dropped the blanket on the ground and pulled it open.

"Now, if I had my knife," Murph said, eyeing the cans, "we could open these."

"Let me show you an old Indian trick," Sam said.

"Oh, no!" Murph said.

Sam grinned and took Murph's knife out of his pocket.

"One thing is for sure," Jim said later, his mouth full of food. "We won't get any help from Mr. Browne."

"You're right, Jim," Sam answered. "We'll have to think of another way to get word to your uncle."

"Mr. Browne isn't the only one at that camp who can help us," Jim said. "Larry Grant is there."

"Who is Larry Grant?" Sam asked.

"Larry Grant works for the rangers. It is his job to watch over the logging."

"He's in with the timber thieves," Murph said.

"Do you know that for sure?" asked Jim.

Murph shook his head. "But why not? If I had a chance to make a little money on the side, I would take it."

"Well, you might," Jim said, "but you're wrong about Larry Grant. Larry Grant is no thief."

"That's what you said about Carl Browne, remember?" Murph said.

Jim fell silent.

"Leave Jim alone," said Sam. "If Larry Grant is in with the others, then why don't they steal from Big Pines during the day. Why wait until night? I have an idea. I think we should go to the logging camp and look things over. Maybe while we're there, we can think of something to do."

On Watch!

The low clouds that had covered Big Pines Forest that morning were lifting as Sam and the boys started their steep climb up the mountain. Though the summer sun was a big yellow ball in the sky, the air was still cool. But by the time Sam and the others were at the top of the ridge, they were warm.

They stopped to catch their breath. Murph pointed to the right. "The cattle rustlers are camped about a mile from here."

As they started down the other side of the ridge, they heard the sound of a caterpillar. The noise grew louder and louder as they made their way to the logging area. They got as close as they could. From behind some pines they watched the loggers, but they could see nothing wrong. Larry Grant seemed to be doing a good, careful job.

Jim put his hand on Sam's arm. "I think we should take a chance on Larry Grant," he whispered. "He's not in with the thieves, I just know it! Mr. Browne is not here. I remember Larry Grant's telling my uncle that Mr. Browne came to work around one. If Mr. Browne stole timber during the night, he would want to sleep in the morning."

Sam had been studying the camp. "Larry Grant never seems to be alone," he whispered. "How will we get a chance to talk to him?"

Jim pointed to a green pickup truck. "That's Larry's pickup. If someone could get near it, he might catch Larry's eye."

Sam looked around the camp again. "That's using your head, Jim. Sooner or later, Larry Grant is going to leave in that truck. I'm going to move down to those rocks at the front of the pickup. From there I might have a chance to talk to Larry without being heard by the loggers."

Jim pointed to some trees just in front of them. "I'm moving closer, too," Jim said. "I'll watch from behind those trees."

"All right, Jim," Sam said. "Murph, circle the camp and get behind that ponderosa pine." Sam pointed to a big tree. "If Larry drives away before I get a chance to talk to him, I want you to run down the road to the next bend. Once around the bend, you'll be able to stop him! Understand?"

"Sure, chief!"

Silently Jim made his way down to the stand of trees. There he waited, watching Grant's every move. From the place behind the trees, he could see Sam. But the redhead was too far away. Just once he caught a short look of Murph's bright red hair.

The day spread before him. The minutes seemed almost like hours. As hard as he tried, he could not keep his eyes open. After a while he dropped off to sleep, the sound of power saws drumming in his ears.

Another kind of sound made Jim wake up. It was the sound of a truck. The driver was Mr. Browne. He drove his pickup truck next to Grant's green one. After parking it, he made his way around the camp to see how the logging was going. As Jim watched, he could hardly believe that Mr. Browne was a thief. Then he remembered his uncle telling him that more and more of the forest was being opened to the tourists. Maybe Mr. Browne felt he should log while he had the chance. Who knew? Still, Jim wished that Murph was wrong about Mr. Browne.

Jim looked over at the tall ponderosa pine. He wondered how Murph was doing. At that very minute, Larry Grant started walking toward the tree.

Larry Grant walked over to the pine and seemed to be studying it. After a while he turned and went back to talk to Mr. Browne. Jim knew they were talking about the tree because Larry Grant was pointing to it. Then one of the loggers came up and started talking to Mr. Browne.

Jim wondered why Murph had not caught Mr. Grant's eye when Larry had been by the tree. Murph had had a good chance.

It was getting harder and harder for Jim to keep his eyes open. Every once in a while he would drop off to sleep.

At last Jim looked at his watch. It would be dark soon. They would have to get Larry's eye soon or it would be too late. Then Larry Grant started toward his green pickup truck.

"Now, Sam," Jim whispered to himself.

As Jim watched, he saw Larry suddenly lift up his head from his logging book and look into the woods. He seemed to be listening. At that minute, Mr. Browne came up.

"Ready to go, Larry?" he asked. "We'll be coming down later. Something seems to be wrong with the cat. I'll have to stay here until it's running right."

Larry nodded his head, took off his hard hat, and threw it inside the pickup. Then he climbed in after it. Minutes later, he was driving down the little winding road.

As the green truck drove around the bend, one of the loggers said, "Where are we logging tonight, Carl?"

"There is a great stand of pine in that canyon up the road," Mr. Browne said. "We'll take out another truck of logs tonight."

The loggers put their saws in the back of the pickups. The man on the caterpillar waved good-by to the others and then headed the big cat up the road. After climbing into the pickups, Mr. Browne and the loggers drove up the road after him.

When the loggers had gone, Sam made his way back to Jim. Then the two of them walked down the road toward the big ponderosa pine.

"Though I really didn't believe Murph," Sam said, "I thought we should go along with him. But Mr. Browne's words have changed my mind. Mr. Browne is stealing timber, all right." Sam looked ahead. "I wonder if Murph was able to stop Larry Grant's pickup?"

As they went by the big pine, Jim grabbed Sam's arm. There was Murph, his back against the tree, his eyes closed. He was sleeping soundly!

Sam gave Murph a sharp push. "What do you mean sleeping, when there is a job to do? You let Grant get away!"

Murph's face grew red. "Why, I—I—"

"I had the same trouble as Murph," Jim cut in. "I could hardly keep my eyes open, too. I went to sleep four or five times."

Sam looked down at the ground. "You're right, Jim, we all could use some sleep. There is no use getting angry at Murph. Larry Grant is gone, and nothing will change that. The thing is—what are we going to do now?"

"I think we should follow Mr. Browne and his men," Jim said. "We should keep our eyes on them."

Sam nodded. "You're right. But I wish there were some way we could get word to the rangers. If today were not Friday, Larry would be coming to work tomorrow. But as it is, he won't be back for three days."

Sam, Jim, and Murph started up the mountain road. As they walked, the sky grew dark. Jim looked up. Again there would be no moon.

They had not gone far when they heard the sounds of power saws. Mr. Browne and his men were already at work!

The three hurried on. Minutes later they were watching silently. Bright lights, hanging from trees, circled the little area. A faller was using a power saw to cut down a white pine. Another logger was cutting a pine into smaller parts. Mr. Browne was helping some men put logs on the big logging truck that was parked across the road.

"Can't we do something?" Jim asked Sam. "Maybe we could let the air out of the tires."

Sam shook his head. "You stay here. I have a better idea. I just remembered an old Indian trick my grandfather showed me."

Jim and Murph watched as Sam circled the camp. When Sam was near one of the pick-ups, he ran to the front. Bending low, he lifted the hood just a little, reached in, and pulled something out.

"Sam is doing something to the trucks so the loggers can't drive away," Jim said.

"I wonder what kind of an old Indian trick Sam was talking about," Murph said. "It can't be too old if it has to do with trucks."

Jim grinned to himself. He wasn't going to tell Murph about Sam's grandfather.

Sam was moving back into the cover of the trees and heading toward another truck.

Just then the faller called, "Timmmmber!"

The loggers stood back and a white pine crashed to the ground.

"Now which one, Carl?" the faller said. Mr. Browne walked over to him. He pointed down the canyon to a good stand of ponderosa pine. "Let's get those next," Mr. Browne said. He turned, walked around the logging truck, and started toward the pickups.

Sam was just putting down a truck's hood. He looked back just as Mr. Browne started toward him. Dropping to the ground, he made his way to the front of the truck. There he lay still. Mr. Browne opened the door of the truck and took out his jacket. Then he turned and started back toward the canyon.

Jim took a deep breath. "I wish there were some way to keep the loggers from cutting those trees," he thought to himself.

"See that gas drum, Murph," Jim said suddenly, pointing to a tank sitting in the back of the pickup that Sam had just left. "That's the gas the loggers use to fill their power saws. If the loggers had no gas for their saws, they couldn't cut down any trees."

"So what is that to me?" asked Murph.

Jim was angry. "Well, if you don't want to stop them, I do. I'm going to drain that gas drum."

Jim looked around to see where Sam was. Sam was heading toward the logging truck. The logging truck was right on the road. There was no cover around it. If anyone looked toward it, Sam would be seen. This was the most dangerous job of all.

Sam was almost to the logging truck when Mr. Browne started toward it, too. Sam dropped to the ground. Mr. Browne's back was to the other trucks.

"Here is my chance," thought Jim.

Slowly and carefully, he started toward the pickup. He made his way slowly along the side of the pickup to the back. He tried not to think of the danger. In minutes he had found the cap to the gas drum.

Jim tried the cap, but he couldn't move it. He looked around. Not far from the truck was

a rock. The boy jumped off the truck, ran over, and picked up the rock. Once back on the truck, he smashed the rock against the cap. The noise he made was covered by the sound of the power saws.

"Oh, oh," Jim thought to himself, his face sharp with worry. Part of the cap had broken off. Maybe he could not get the cap off now.

Just then there was a shout. "Hey! Who is there!" Mr. Browne's voice was sharp.

Jim turned around. Mr. Browne was coming toward him, his black pipe moving up and down in his mouth. Jim tried the cap again. It came off! The gas started to run out of the drum into the back of the truck. Just as the cap came off, Mr. Browne grabbed Jim's jacket and pulled the boy back. With his other hand, he reached for the cap.

Carl Browne had no sooner grabbed the cap, when someone grabbed him. Murph had slipped up behind him. Murph put his hand under Mr. Browne's chin and started to pull him back. But Murph did not think about the ribs he had hurt in the fall down the mountain. As he pulled at Mr. Browne, he cried out with pain.

Mr. Browne turned, his face bright red. He punched Murph in the side, and the boy went down. Murph had blacked out!

Jim jumped on Mr. Browne, punching him in the back. The logger pulled him off.

"You smart kid!" the logger said, "I'll make you pay for—"

His hand, hard as a rock, swung toward Jim's face.

Jim put his head down, and Mr. Browne's closed hand punched the air.

Then Jim had an idea. Quickly he reached into his pocket, pulled out the can of spray paint, and pointed it at Mr. Browne's face.

At the camp of the cattle rustlers, things were not going very well. As Murph had said, the two rustlers could not get off of Woodman's Ridge. They could not leave at night because Mr. Browne was cutting timber.

When the rustlers woke up and found that the food they had stolen from Eagle Pass was gone, they did not know what to think. Someone or something had made off with their food. But who—or what? That was it! They had had it. They were getting out! They were getting out tonight!

"Now, Pete," the man in the blue jacket said, "you know what you have to do."

The man named Pete nodded his head. "That logging truck is blocking the road. If I can get it off the road, you can drive the cattle truck through. All we need is a minute or two."

The other man said, "It should work. Now after you get in the logging truck and start the engine, lay your hand on that horn. When I hear the horn, I'll start the cattle truck. Browne and his men will think that we are the rangers. They should be too surprised to move. When you drive that logging truck off the road, I'll drive the cattle truck through. I'll slow down just enough for you to jump in, all right?"

Pete said, "It has to work, that's all!"

The two rustlers jumped into the cattle truck and started down the ridge road. As they neared the timber camp, they could hear the noise of the power saws. Around the bend from the camp, the rustlers stopped.

Pete got out and made his way carefully through the trees to the logging truck. Quietly he opened the door. He tried the engine and put his hand on the horn.

Indian Signs

Just as the horn went off, Jim sprayed Mr. Browne in the face with the can of yellow paint. Jim stared in surprise. For a minute he thought the sound came from his can of paint. Then he knew it was a horn. He looked toward the logging truck.

Pete could not start the logging truck. But the other cattle rustler had come around the bend with the cattle truck. When he tried to drive it through, he found the logging truck in the middle of the road. He couldn't get around it, and he was going too fast to stop. There was only one thing to do. He drove the cattle truck off the road. It landed against a tree and almost turned over. The side of the truck gave way, and the cattle started jumping out and running through the logging camp.

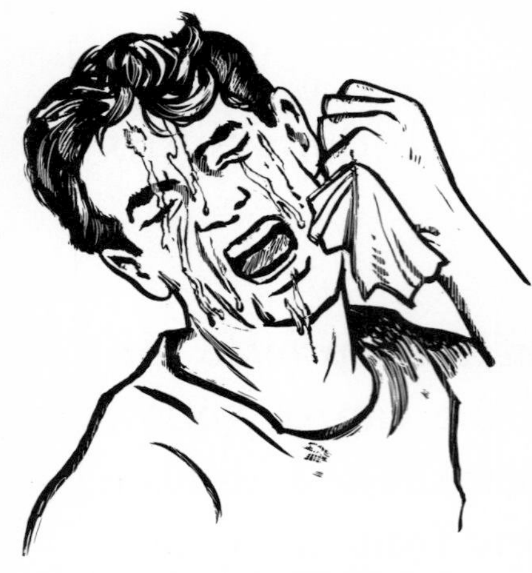

All this had happened in just minutes. All the while, Mr. Browne had been trying to get the paint off his face. Jim hardly looked at him. He just stared at the cattle running through camp.

Mr. Browne had found his voice at last. "Let's get out of here," he cried. "The rangers are coming!"

His words were wasted. The loggers had already dropped their tools and had run for the pickups, but not one truck would start. The loggers wasted no time in making tracks into the forest. The cattle rustlers had already gone.

Suddenly Sam was at Jim's side, his hand on Mr. Browne's arm. "Sir!" he ordered, his voice cold, "you had better stand quietly. I'll tell you only once that I know judo very well, and you have no chance to get away."

Murph was coming to. His face was white as he tried to get up.

"Go away," he said, pushing away Sam's other hand. "I can get up without your help."

Murph stood up. He was in pain, but he tried not to show it.

"What happened?" he wanted to know.

Quickly Jim and Sam told him.

"We'll have to get out of here, Sam," Jim said. "What if the loggers come back looking for Mr. Browne!"

"I don't think so, Jim," Sam said and laughed. "They are running so fast that they won't think of looking back."

Murph was grinning. "What a wild time!" he said. "I wish I had seen it!"

Mr. Browne said nothing.

"Do you think you can make it back to the cabin, Murph?" Sam wanted to know. "We'll have to take turns watching this timber rustler until we can get some help, but I have no idea how we're going to do it."

"Don't tell me the big chief is all out of bright ideas," Murph said. "Tell me, what would your Indian grandfather do?"

"If he was smart," Jim put in, "he would get some sleep."

Sam shook his head and grinned. "Go ahead, make fun. But an Indian can get help with just a fire or a blanket."

"So there are blankets back at the cabin—so what?" Murph said. "Just who is going to see them. Not just anyone can understand Indian signs. It takes another Indian to know what they mean!"

Jim's eyes were bright. He looked up at the sky. There was not a cloud to be seen.

"Tomorrow *will* be a good day. There won't be a cloud in the sky. After the clouds this morning, Uncle Don will have to fly over Big Pines Forest again tomorrow in the helicopter. And Sam!"—Jim turned to the tall, tan young man—"Ranger Don's pilot is an Indian!"

The next morning the ranger was looking over the side of the helicopter. For the last hour, he and his pilot, Bud Young, had been flying over Big Pines Forest. Now they were over the road to Eagle Pass.

"See any signs of cattle rustlers?" asked Bud.

"None at all," said the ranger.

"Well, Woodman's Ridge is the only part of the forest left, ranger. Then we can head back to the ranger station."

"We're close to the cabin, Bud. I want to get a good look at our young men. They should be out cutting gooseberry bushes by now."

"Ranger!" Bud called out. "Look down there. Isn't that Jim and another boy?"

Looking down, the ranger couldn't believe what he saw.

"Jumping cats, Bud, get a little closer. What are they doing?"

Sam was waving a blanket in front of him, up and down, up and down. And Jim! Jim was waving a blanket above his head and running around in circles.

Bud laughed. "Looks as though they are having fun, ranger—more fun than cutting gooseberry bushes!"

"Put the helicopter down, Bud. I'll tell them a thing or two! Clowning around when they should be working! That's not like Jim!"

As the helicopter started down, the ranger saw Jim falling, still holding the blanket.

Or—the ranger wasn't sure—the blanket was holding Jim. Jim was having trouble getting up. If the ranger had not been so angry, he would have laughed.

As soon as the helicopter reached the ground, the ranger jumped out. He rushed to Jim. "What is the meaning of all this?"

Jim sat up and pushed the blanket away.

"Uncle Don, the blanket waved up and down means for you to stop. The blanket waved around in a circle means that I've found something." Jim looked at the pilot. "Bud, you're an Indian. Why don't you know Indian signs?"

Bud shook his head. "I grew up in the city, Jim. I can't even make a fire. I—"

"Never mind that!" the ranger broke in. "Jim, tell me what is wrong."

"Let's go inside the cabin," Sam said. "Murph has someone there you should meet."

They all went into the cabin, where Murph was watching Mr. Browne.

"Good morning, sir," Murph said.

Jim shook his head. He didn't think he could stand it. Gone was Murph's fast, smart talk. There was a friendly smile on Murph's face as he talked to the ranger.

"Mr. Browne has a lot of things to tell you." The redhead pushed Mr. Browne toward the ranger.

Mr. Browne didn't feel like talking, so Sam, Jim, and Murph did it for him.

"And so, Uncle Don," Jim finished, "we came back to the cabin and watched Mr. Browne until we heard your helicopter. Then Sam showed me how to wave the blanket."

The pilot laughed. "Your uncle and I thought you were clowning around, trying to get out of cutting gooseberry bushes."

"Jumping cats!" the ranger said. "I should be angry with you for taking so many chances. You did some dangerous things." Then he grinned. "Which way were the rustlers running when you last saw them?"

Sam grinned back. "Every way."

"I'll call the main ranger station and tell them what you have told me," Ranger Don said. "We have to get Murph back and have someone look at his ribs. And there is a good strong jail in Two Rivers, just right for you," he added to Mr. Browne. "But you two"—the ranger looked at Jim and Sam—"have a job."

Jim said. "Not those gooseberry bushes!"

"Yes," the ranger said.

Later, as Jim watched the helicopter fly away, he said, "I don't know about you, Sam, but I could use some sleep."

A big smile crossed Sam's tan face. "Come on, Jim. You had one hour of sleep the first night up here. And you had one hour last night. You want to sleep all the time?"

Jim grinned. "Very funny, Sam. Where are those tools?"

Big Pines

The next day the ranger and Murph picked up Sam and Jim at Eagle Pass. Then the four drove to Woodman's Ridge.

Murph's ribs had not been broken in the fall. Murph could not do any hard work for five days, but after that he would be all right.

The law had picked up all the rustlers. Murph had been a lot of help. He had pointed out the cattle rustlers and all the loggers who had been stealing trees from the forest. Later, when the men would come before a judge, Sam, Jim, and Murph would have to be there, too.

The ranger pulled the pickup to a stop, and they all got out. Mr. Browne's logging truck and the pickups were still there.

"We'll have to get a mechanic up here before we can get these trucks out. Sam, you did a good job keeping the rustlers from starting their trucks."

"Just what was that old Indian trick your grandfather showed you?" Murph asked.

"Well,"—Sam grinned—"my grandfather did show me that little trick, but it is not an Indian trick. Any good mechanic can do it."

Sam saw that Murph did not understand. "I've just been kidding you. My grandfather never lived on a reservation. Both of us grew up in a city. All the Indian tricks I know, I learned from books. Why, when it comes to living in the country, my grandfather knows about as much as the ranger's pilot does!"

"And that's not much," Jim said.

The ranger was walking around the logging area. He shook his head as he looked at the felled trees and broken branches.

"Carl Browne was smart," the ranger said. "He and his men would log with Larry Grant all day. Then at night, they would come up here and take out a few more trees. They had all the things they needed right here—a caterpillar, a logging truck, tools.

"If they had waited until you boys had finished cutting out gooseberries, they might never have been caught. But Carl Browne didn't want to wait until you had gone. That's why he and one of his men drove up to Eagle Pass the first night you were there. They wanted to find out if you could hear them if they logged at night. But you heard their truck and went looking for them."

"And Murph followed the cattle rustlers and found out what was going on," Jim put in.

The ranger laughed.

"What is so funny, Uncle Don?" Jim asked.

"I was just thinking of your spraying Carl Browne with a can of paint," said the ranger.

"I've heard of marked men, but this is the first time I ever heard of marking one with paint.

"Well, the timber rustlers and the cattle rustlers are in jail and they won't be able to steal for some time. Now we have to think about what we're going to do here."

The ranger started walking down the canyon. Suddenly he stopped. "Jumping cats!" he said.

Jim turned to look at his uncle. There was a funny look on the ranger's face.

"What is it, Uncle Don?" Jim asked.

The ranger pushed back his hat and pointed down the canyon. There was a stand of ponderosa pine. The trees stood tall and straight. They rose far up in the blue sky.

"Those trees are really tall, aren't they, sir?" Sam asked.

"They sure are! And I think they are even taller than they look. See how low the canyon is? Those pines might be the tallest trees in the whole forest. But even if they aren't, they are the best-looking trees that I have ever seen.

"No one has ever seen them before because there were other pines in front. But when Mr. Browne cut down the trees in this part of the canyon, he left that part open."

Then the ranger thought of something. "If you three had not stopped Mr. Browne when you did, he would have cut down all these pines. We never would have known that these great trees were in Big Pines."

"People will want to come here to see these trees," Jim said. "We'll have to get to work. All these branches will have to come out."

The ranger nodded. "I have some other ideas that I want to try out here."

"I hope that I am around to help, too, ranger," Sam said.

Murph was staring at the pines, too. The wild look in his eyes was gone. "I—I would like to help, too," he said.

"Oh, oh," Jim thought to himself. "Murph feels the same as we do about the pines. I can't believe it!" Jim thought back to his first meeting with the redhead. What was it Murph had said—something about not wasting his life watching over a bunch of trees?

Out loud, Jim said, "This part of the forest is good for many things." He grinned. "If you have strong feet, it is good for walking."

"It is good for tracking and camping, too," Sam said, caught up in the fun.

"How about swimming—it's good for that, too!" Murph put in. "By the way, Sam, would you mind showing me how to swim?"

"I sure will," Sam said, "if you show me how to track. I sure would like to learn."

Jim cut in. "Would one of you mind showing me just one judo throw? That's something I would like to learn."

The ranger smiled and moved down the canyon toward the tall pines. He knew that the three friends had a lot to talk about.

EXERCISES

Chapter One

A CLOSE CALL

Make It Right

Choose the right word or words for each sentence. Then write the sentence on your paper.

1. ________ shouted, "Look out!"
   (Ranger Don) (Carl Browne) (Jim)
2. Blister rust grows on ________.
   (boulders) (gooseberry bushes) (cattle)
3. The loggers were to cut the trees marked with ________.
   (branches) (yellow paint) (white circles)
4. ________ measured and marked logs.
   (Ranger Don) (Carl Browne) (Larry Grant)
5. People pay a lot of money for ________.
   (ponderosa pine) (white pine) (branches)
6. Jim wanted to be a ________.
   (logger) (rancher) (ranger)
7. Ranger Don sent Jim to ________.
   (Two Rivers) (Eagle Pass) (Wood Ridge)
8. Ranger Don was going to look for ________.
   (forest fires) (rustlers) (tourists)

Chapter Two

JIM MEETS MURPH

Which Is Right?

Read each sentence below. Does the chapter you have read say it is true? On your paper, write only those sentences that are true.

1. Jim liked Murph right away.
2. Murph called Sam an old man.
3. Sam, Murph, and Jim were going to pull up gooseberry bushes at Eagle Pass.
4. Sam's grandfather was an Indian.
5. Murph's mother sent him to Big Pines Forest.
6. Jim was shorter and smaller than Murph.
7. Murph used a judo trick on Sam.
8. Jim found only men's clothes in the cabin.
9. The fire-fighting tools were missing.

Let's Talk About It

1. Why was it important for Sam and the boys to pull up *all* the gooseberry bushes?
2. What are some of the things Murph could learn in the forest?

Chapter Three

A TRUCK COMES TO EAGLE PASS

Go-together Words

On your paper, write the pairs of words that go together.

rustlers-thieves	quiet-whisper
jacket-engine	watch-see
bed-bunk	tracks-radio
cup-tourist	flashlight-cattle

What Happened First?

Each of these things happened in the chapter you have just read, but they are mixed up here. On your paper, write them as they happened.

1. Jim stepped on a dry branch.
2. Sam heard the sound of an engine.
3. The smashed radio was found.
4. Murph crept away into the forest.
5. The men with a flashlight came toward Jim and Sam.
6. A man in a blue jacket ran off through the forest.

Chapter Four

GOING FOR HELP

WHO DID IT?

On your paper, write the name of the person or persons that answers each question.

1. Whose knife lay on Sam's bunk?
2. Who started to go to the ranger station?
3. Whose camp is on Woodman's Ridge?
4. Who said, "Someone has drained the tank"?
5. Who once climbed a pine tree and stayed up there all night?
6. Who said, "Let's cut across the mountain"?
7. Who said he understood Murph, but he still got angry at him?

LET'S TALK ABOUT IT

1. If Murph were lost in the forest, how might he be in danger?
2. How do you know that Sam and Jim like the forest?
3. What kind of life did Murph have before he came to Big Pines Forest?

Chapter Five
SMOKE AND CLOUDS

WHAT HAPPENED FIRST?

Each of these happened in the chapter you have just read, but they are mixed up here. On your paper, write them as they happened.

1. The men heard the noise from a helicopter.
2. Murph said that he couldn't swim.
3. Jim and Sam threw wet wood on the fire.
4. Jim and Sam started downstream without Murph.
5. Sam showed Murph how to lie back in the water.
6. Jim and Sam heard Murph calling for help.

GO-TOGETHER WORDS

On your paper, write the pairs of words that go together.

needles-pine
blue-dry
tan-sun
fall-slip
chief-square
pain-cloud
tough-wide
bottom-across

Chapter Six

RUSTLERS

WHICH IS RIGHT?

Read each sentence below. Does the chapter you have read say it is true? On your paper, write only those sentences that are true.

1. Murph smashed the radio.
2. The man in the blue jacket was Mr. Browne.
3. The rustlers stole food from the cabin.
4. Sam followed the signs that Murph had left.
5. The men in the truck were rangers.
6. The rustlers were camped near a canyon.
7. Murph stole the food back from the rustlers.
8. Sam and the boys went back to Eagle Pass.
9. Murph knew Larry Grant was no thief.
10. Jim remembered the smell of Grant's pipe.

TO THINK ABOUT

1. Why, do you think, does a ranger work with the loggers in a forest?
2. Do you think Murph is beginning to like Big Pines Forest? Give reasons for your answer.

Chapter Seven

ON WATCH!

WHO DID IT?

Number your paper from 1 to 7. Write the name of the person or persons that answers the question.

1. Who hid in the rocks in front of the pickup?
2. Who was supposed to stop Larry Grant after he had driven around the bend?
3. Who wanted to empty the gas drum?
4. Who pulled something from under the hood of a pickup?
5. Who fell asleep?
6. Who grabbed Carl Browne from behind?
7. Who drove towards the logging camp?

GO-TOGETHER WORDS

On your paper, write the pairs of words that go together.

morning-area	noise-sound
wood-timber	silent-danger
truck-pickup	spray-block
bend-camp	hurt-pain

Chapter Eight

INDIAN SIGNS

WHICH IS RIGHT?

Read each sentence below. Does the chapter you have read say it is true? On your paper, write only those sentences that are true.

1. Mr. Browne drove the cattle truck.
2. The pickup trucks had flat tires.
3. Murph said that he was in pain.
4. Ranger Don's pilot was an Indian.
5. Murph was ready to use judo on Mr. Browne.
6. Ranger Don thought that Jim and Sam were playing when he first saw them.
7. Mr. Browne told Ranger Don the story of the timber rustlers.
8. There was a jail in Two Rivers.
9. Jim and Sam stayed in the forest to watch for the cattle rustlers.

TO THINK ABOUT AND TALK ABOUT

Do you think Sam and Jim will make good forest rangers? Give reasons for your answer.

Chapter Nine

BIG PINES

Which One Said It?

Which one of the people in the story said each of these sentences? You may look at the chapter.

1. "Those pines might be the tallest trees in the whole forest."
2. "This part of the forest is good for many things."
3. "I—I would like to help, too."
4. "Would one of you mind showing me just one judo throw?"
5. "We never would have known that these great trees were in Big Pines."
6. "Both of us grew up in a city."
7. "And Murph followed the cattle rustlers and found out what was going on."

To Think About and Talk About

1. How has Murph changed since Jim met him?
2. How can you tell that Ranger Don likes Big Pines Forest?

WORD LIST

The total number of running words in *Jim Forest and Woodman's Ridge* is 13,871, and the number of different words used is 600. Of these, 539 should be familiar to children reading at the third-grade level. The remaining 61 words, which are above third-grade level but necessary to the context of the story, are listed below according to the page on which they first occur.

vi	boulder	18	chief	53	—
	cloud		jail	54	—
	ranger	19	grab	55	—
	shiny		punch	56	—
	silent		reservation	57	—
	study		ribs	58	—
	that's	20	—	59	—
1	rustler	21	bunk	60	—
	smash		sink	61	thieving
	television	22	—	62	—
2	blister	23	redhead	63	—
	logger	24	judo	64	—
	rust	25	—	65	—
	spray	26	—	66	—
3	gooseberry	27	tough	67	—
4	pickup	28	flashlight	68	—
	ridge	29	—	69	—
5	job	30	tourists	70	—
6	canyon	31	—	71	—
	faller	32	—	72	—
7	area	33	—	73	—
8	—	34	idea	74	—
9	important	35	—	75	—
	waste	36	—	76	—
10	ponderosa	37	—	77	—
	timber	38	—	78	—
11	forestry	39	mechanic	79	—
	graze	40	tank	80	—
	rancher	41	drain	81	—
12	helicopter	42	steep	82	—
13	fifty	43	—	83	—
	stolen	44	—	84	pilot
14	tan	45	downstream	85	—
15	understand	46	—	86	—
16	crazy	47	—	87	—
	he's	48	—	88	—
	sonny	49	—	89	—
17	judge	50	—	90	—
	smart	51	—	91	—
	yeah	52	pain	92	—

HONEYWELL GRADE SCHOOL